Amazing Animal
Hide and Seek

For JJ . . . the best

Amazing Animal Hide and Seek

JOHN ROWE

BARRON'S

We are:

Cat and Bat,
Hare and Bear,
Duck and Goose,
Frog and Hog,
and Mouse and Moose.

We're looking for a finder for
our game of hide and seek,
and we wondered if you'd
like to play. Yes?

Well, shut your eyes and
count to ten.
And make sure that you don't peek!

We're off!

one

two

three

four

five

six

seven

eight

nine

ten

COMING!

Who is hiding in the field?

He's sleek and white,
with paws and claws.

When you've found him,
turn the page.

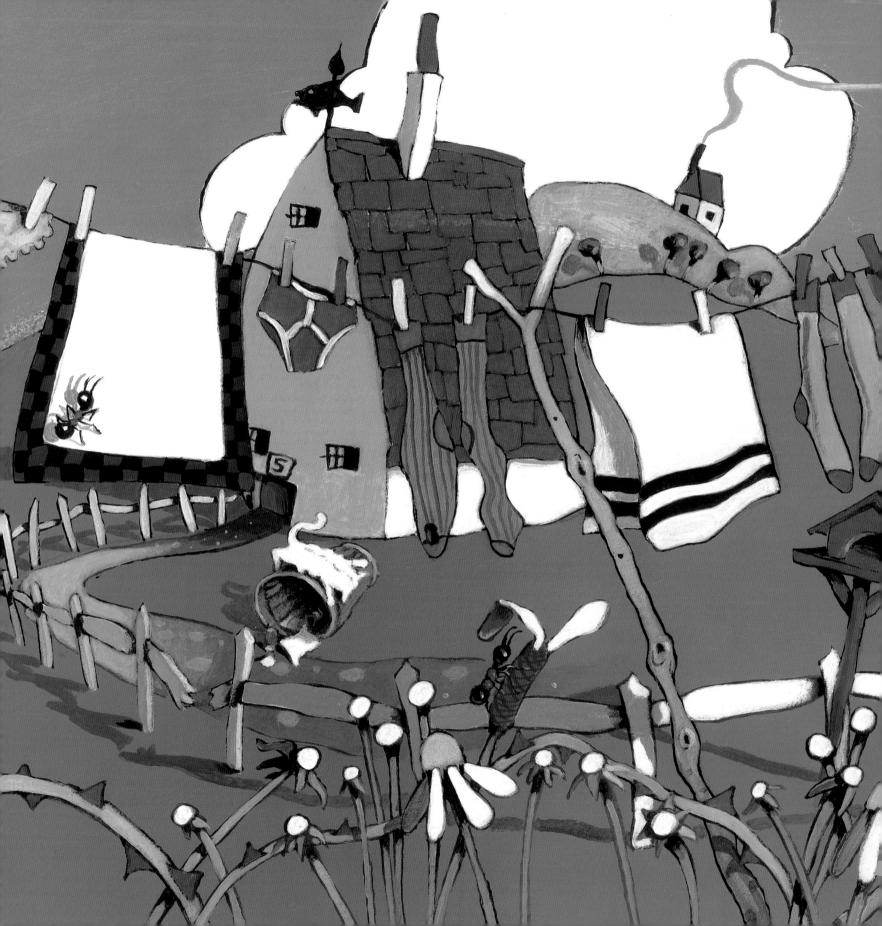

Well done!

You've found that **CAT**.

Now who is hiding in the yard?

He hangs around
upside down.

When you've found him,
turn the page.

Well done!

You've found that **BAT**.

Now who is hiding in the meadow?

Her ears are long, and
she bounds along.

When you've found her,
turn the page.

Well done!

You've found that **HARE**.

Now who is hiding in the forest?

He lumbers and roars, and
has great big paws.

When you've found him,
turn the page.

Well done!

You've found that **BEAR**.

Now who is hiding in the reeds?

He swims and waddles
and quacks and paddles.

When you've found him,
turn the page.

Well done!

You've found that **DUCK**.

Now who is hiding near the house?

She's soft and feathery, and
she wobbles and gobbles.

When you've found her,
turn the page.

Well done!

You've found that **GOOSE**.

Who is hiding in the water?

"Croak! Croak! Croak!" he goes, and has little webs between his toes.

When you've found him, turn the page.

Well done!

You've found that **FROG**.

Who is hiding by the barn?

He's covered in warts, and
snuffles and snorts.

When you've found him,
turn the page.

Well done!

You've found that **HOG**.

Now who is hiding in
the thicket?

He's a bit like a horse, but instead
has great big antlers on his head.

When you've found him,
turn the page.

Well done!
You've found that **MOOSE**.

Who is hiding in the house?

He squeaks and twitches,
and scurries and hurries.

He's so tiny, will you ever find him?
Will you tiptoe up behind him?
Is he here or is he there?
Is he hiding anywhere?

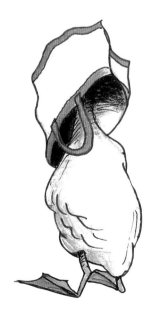

The last one left has won the game.

Who is it?
Who could the winner be?
Why don't you try the door
and see . . .

AMAZING ANIMAL HIDE AND SEEK
A HUTCHINSON BOOK

First edition for the United States, its territories and dependencies,
and Canada published in 2003 by Barron's Educational Series, Inc.

Published in Great Britain by Hutchinson,
an imprint of Random House Children's Books

All inquiries should be addressed to:
Barron's Educational Series, Inc.
250 Wireless Boulevard
Hauppauge, New York 11788
http://www.barronseduc.com

International Standard Book No. 0-7641-5667-5

Library of Congress Catalog Card No. 2002116531

Printed and bound in Malaysia by Tien Wah Press [PTE] Ltd
9 8 7 6 5 4 3 2 1